T. REX TIME MACHINE

JARED CHAPMAN

chronicle books · san francisco

One day a time traveler traveled back to prehistoric times . . .
Hey look, food.

which he quickly regretted.

So much work for such little meat.
Tell me about it.
What is this thing?
Beats me, but I think I smell food inside.

The dinosaurs curiously
climbed aboard . . .
Save me some.

and were flung far into the future.

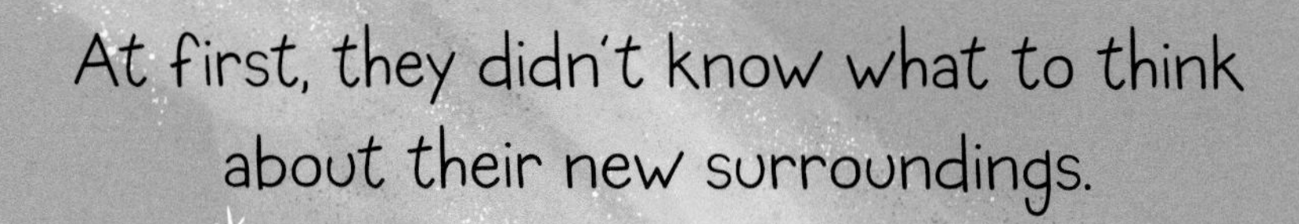

At first, they didn't know what to think about their new surroundings.

But they soon got the hang of it.

Tastes like Pteranodon.

CHEW
CHEW
CHEW
I need a pizza delivered to the convenience store on Main Street.

AGH! MONSTERS!
The pizza's on the way.

Are you seeing what I'm seeing?
WATER
ICE
DELI
OPEN 24 Hrs

TACOS
Cafe
BAKERY
FEST

SUB CITY

TODAY!
annual
DONUT FESTIVAL

There's tacos!

And subs!

And cakes!

And more!

FOOD IS EVERYWHERE!

What is that?
See you in a few, delicious noodles.

WHHHHHIIIII
3:00

IIIIRRRRRRRRR
2:30

RRRRRLLLLLLLL
2:00

You order the pizza?
Wow.

WHHHIIIIIIIIIIIIRRRRRRRRRLLLLLLLL
1:30

The dinosaurs
were scared.

But just then . . .
DONE
POP!
NOODLE
DING!

EVERYBODY GET DOWN!
OLICE

PO LICE
PO
Let's get out of here!

annual
DONUT FESTIVAL
Donut?
Yes, please!
No time!
This way!

The dinosaurs were running out of time.
They needed to get home fast.

Let's just get back to that magic egg!

But their problems weren't over.

We don't know how to make this thing go!

The dinosaurs were stuck. They were sad

They threw a huge tantrum.

I didn't get a donut!

I want to go home!

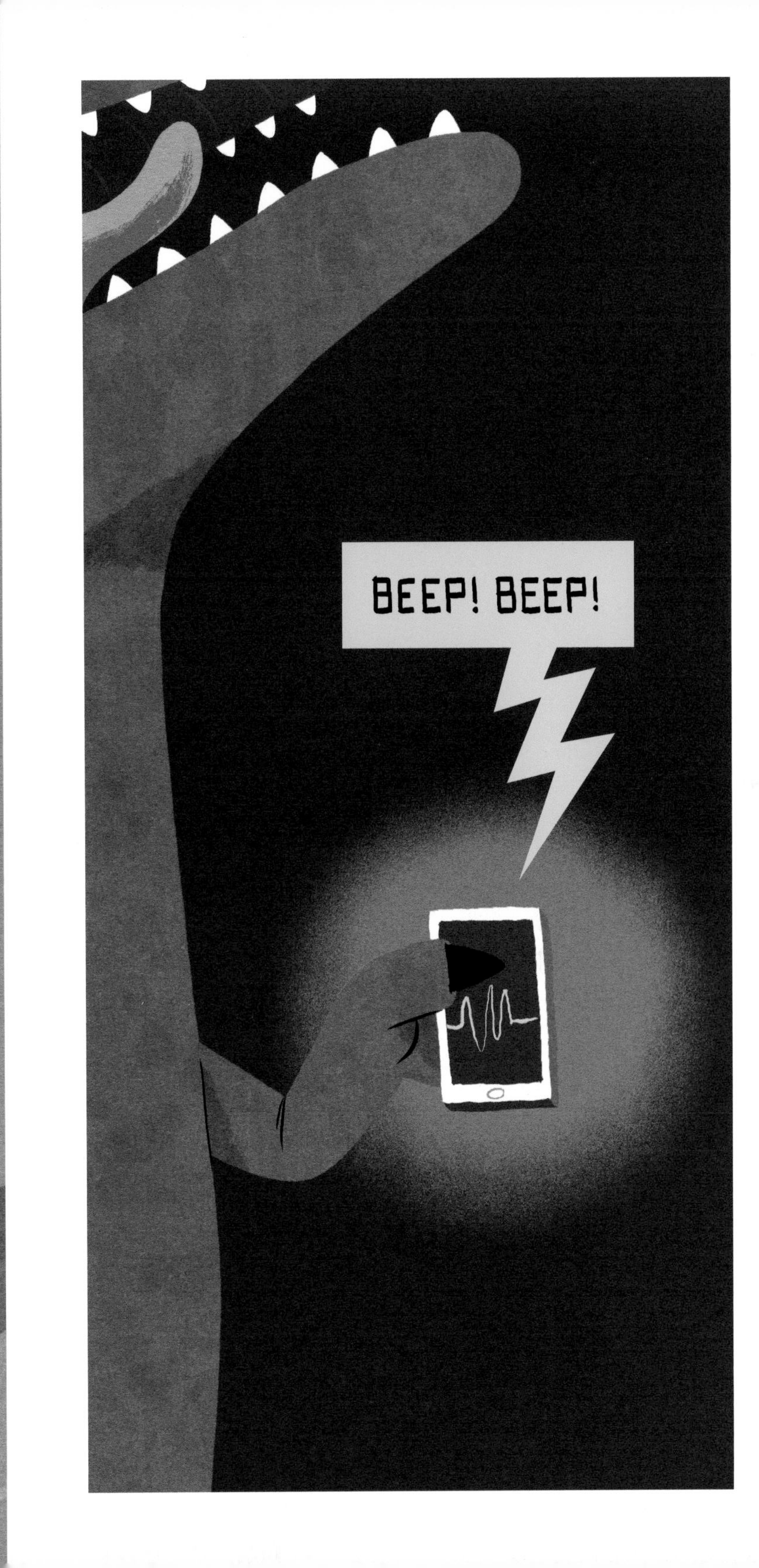
BEEP! BEEP!

I missed my CHANCE at a doNUT!
I didn't quite get that.
Did you say...

"I want to dance with King Tut"?
NOOOOO!

I don't know who this Tut guy is, but he'd better have a donut.

For Amanda.
Past, present, future.

Library of Congress Cataloging-in-Publication Data:

ISBN 978-1-4521-6154-9

Manufactured in China.

Design by Ryan Hayes.
Lettering by Jared Chapman.
Typeset in Coop Forged.
The illustrations in this book came from a future time where they will be created digitally using a sophisticated and mysterious Science.

10 9 8 7 6 5 4 3 2

Chronicle Books LLC
680 Second Street
San Francisco, California 94107

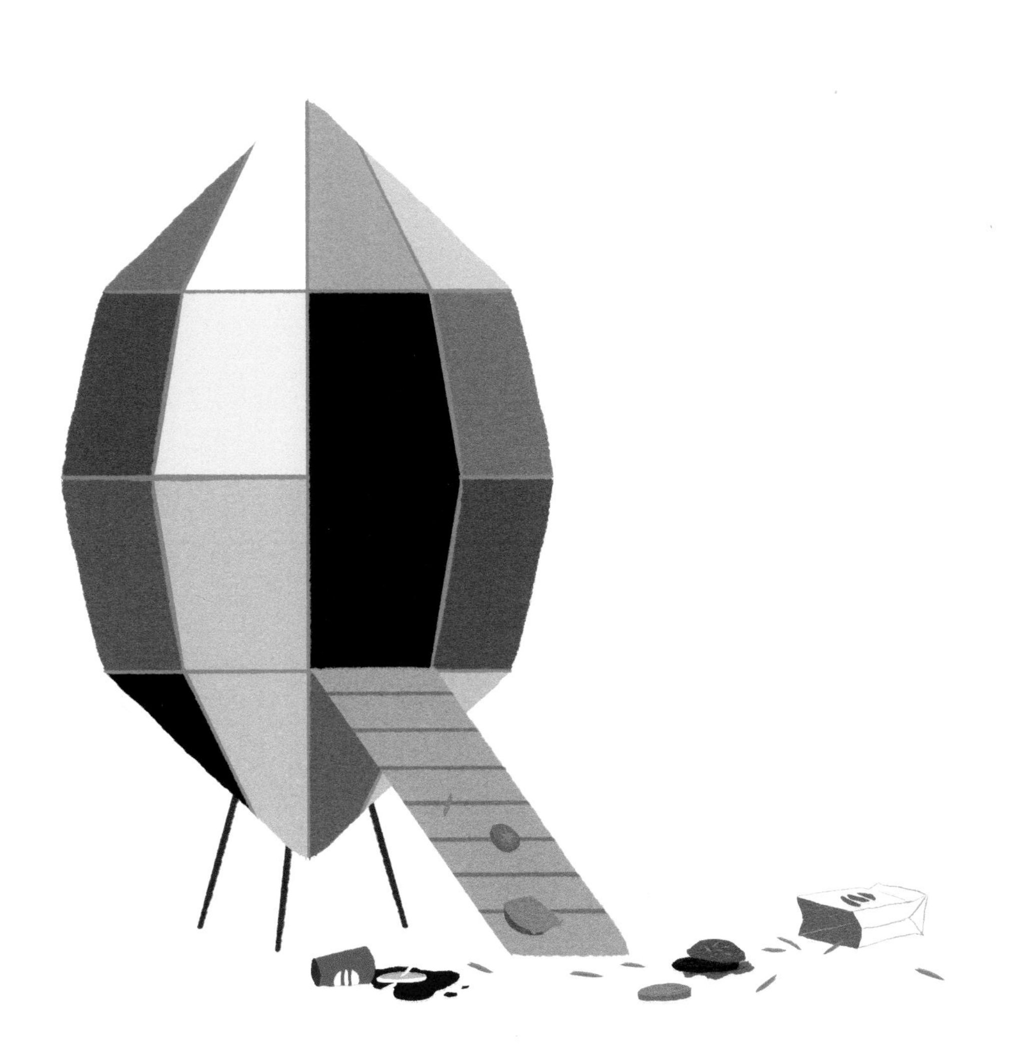